J.G. Holland

The Mistress of the Manse, a Poem

J.G. Holland

The Mistress of the Manse, a Poem

ISBN/EAN: 9783744708067

Printed in Europe, USA, Canada, Australia, Japan

Cover: Foto ©Andreas Hilbeck / pixelio.de

More available books at **www.hansebooks.com**

THE

MISTRESS OF THE MANSE

DR. J. G. HOLLAND'S WRITINGS.

Complete Works. 16 Volumes. Small 12mo.
Sold separately.

BITTER-SWEET,	$1.25
KATHRINA,	1.25
THE MISTRESS OF THE MANSE,	1.25
PURITAN'S GUEST AND OTHER POEMS,	1.25
TITCOMB'S LETTERS TO YOUNG PEOPLE,	1.25
GOLD-FOIL,	1.25
LESSONS IN LIFE,	1.25
PLAIN TALKS ON FAMILIAR SUBJECTS,	1.25
CONCERNING THE JONES FAMILY,	1.25
EVERY-DAY TOPICS. FIRST SERIES,	1.25
" " SECOND SERIES,	1.25
SEVENOAKS,	1.25
THE BAY PATH,	1.25
ARTHUR BONNICASTLE,	1.25
MISS GILBERT'S CAREER,	1.25
NICHOLAS MINTURN,	1.25

Complete Sets, 16 vols., in a box: half calf, $44.00; half morocco, gilt top, $46.00; and cloth, $20.00.

CAMEO EDITION.

BITTER-SWEET. With an etching by OTTO BACHER. 16mo, ... $1.25
KATHRINA. With an etching by A. M. TURNER. 16mo, 1.25
The Set, 2 vols. in a box: half calf, gilt top, $5.50; half morocco, $7.00; cloth, $2.50.

COMPLETE POETICAL WRITINGS.

With illustrations by Reinhart, Griswold, and Mary Hallock Foote, and a portrait by Wyatt Eaton. 8vo, $3.50.

THE

MISTRESS OF THE MANSE

A POEM

BY

J. G. HOLLAND

NEW YORK
CHARLES SCRIBNER'S SONS
1897

CONTENTS.

THE

MISTRESS OF THE MANSE.

PRELUDE.

In all the crowded Universe

There is but one stupendous Word;

And huge and rough, or trimmed and terse,

Its fragments build and undergird

The songs and stories we rehearse.

All forms that human language tries,

All phrases of the books and schools,

And all the words of great and wise

Are weak attempts, or clumsy tools,

To speak the Word that speech defies.

The Mistress of the Manse.

That Word, ineffable to man,
Though whispered through a thousand years,
Or thundered in the fiery van
Of all the myriad-wheeling spheres,
Remains unvoiced since time began.

There is no tree that rears its crest,
No fern or flower that cleaves the sod,
Nor bird that sings above its nest,
But tries to speak this Word of God,
And dies when it has done its best.

Like marble in the mountain mine,
White at its heart as on its face,
We chip its crystals, nor divine
The forms of majesty and grace
That wait within the central shrine!

The Mistress of the Manse.

And this Great Word, all words above,
Including, yet defying all—
Soft as the crooning of a dove,
And strong as the Archangel's call—
Means only this—means only Love!

It represents Creation's whole,—
All space, all worlds, all living things :
And Love endows them with a soul,—
The bright Shechinah, throned in wings
Behind the Temple's Sacred Scroll!

The love of home and native land,
The love that springs in son and sire,
And that which welds the heart and hand
Of man and maiden in its fire,
Are signs by which we understand

The love whose passion shook The Cross;

And all those loves that, deep and broad,

Make princely gain of piteous loss,

Reveal the love that lives in God

As in a blood-illumined gloss.

II.

Mayhap the humble tale I tell

Of the great passion which absorbs

The gentle hearts that round me dwell,

And wings the world, and holds the orbs,

And strews the skies with asphodel,

Will yield some letters of the Word

Which still unspoken must remain;

And bear to bosoms, swelled and stirred,

Some meanings of the tender pain

Which they have neither seen nor heard·

The Mistress of the Manse.

My Philip, bred in Northern climes,
Preached the great Word I strive to sing;
And in the grand and golden times—
Aflame with love—he went to bring
His Mildred—subject of my rhymes—

From her far home on Southern plains;
And what they shared of bale and bliss,
And what their losses, what their gains,
The loving eye that readeth this
May gather, if it take the pains.

LOVE'S EXPERIMENTS.

I.

THE group of ladies at the gate
Dissolved, and tripped in haste away;
And then, with backward tilting freight,
The old stage coach, in dusty gray,
Stopped; and the pastor and his mate

Stepped forth, and passed the waiting door,
And closed it on the gazing street.
"Oh, Philip!" She could say no more;
"Oh, Mildred! You're at home, my sweet,—
The old life closed: the new before!"

" Dinah, the mistress ! " · And the maid,

Grown motherly with household care

And loving service, and arrayed

In homely neatness, took the pair

Of small gloved hands held out, and paid

Her low obeisance ; then—" this way ! "

And when she brought her forth at last,

To him who grudged the long delay,

He found the soil of travel cast,

And Mildred fresh and fair as May.

II.

" This is our little Manse," he said ;

" Now look with both your curious eyes

Around, beneath, and overhead,

And, seeing all things, realize

That they are ours, and we are wed !

" Walk through these freshly garnished rooms—
These halls of oak and tinted pearl ;
And mark the cups of clover-blooms,
Cut fresh, to greet the stranger-girl,
By those whose courtesy illumes

"The house beyond the grace of flowers !
They greet you, mantled by my name,
And rain their tenderness in showers ;
Responding to the double claim
Of love no longer mine, but ours.

" This is our parlor, plain and sweet :
Your hands shall make it half divine.
That wide, old-fashioned window-seat,
Beneath your touch shall grow a shrine ;
And every nooklet and retreat,

The Mistress of the Manse.

"And every barren ledge and shelf,

Shall wear a charm beyond the boon

Of treasure-bearing drift, or delf,

Or dreams that flutter from the moon;

For it shall blossom with yourself.

"This is my study: here, alone,

Prayerful to Him whom I adore,

And gathering speech to make him known,

Your far, quick footsteps on the floor,

Your breezy robe, your cheerful tone,

"As through our pretty home you speed

The busy ministries of life,

Shall stir me swifter than my creed,

And be more musical, dear wife,

Than sweep of harp, or pipe of reed.

1*

" Here is our fairy banquet hall!
See how it opens to the East,
And looks through elms! The board is small,
But what it bears shall be a feast
At morn, at noon, and evenfall.

"There will you sit in girlish grace,
And catch the sunrise in your hair;
And looking at you, from my place,
I shall behold more sweet and fair,
The morning, in your smiling face!

"And guests shall come, and guests shall go,
And break with us our daily bread;
And sometime—sometime—do you know?
I hope that—dearest, lift your head,
And let me speak it, soft and low!

" The grass is sweeter than the ground :

Can love be finer than its flowers ?

Oh, sometime—sometime—in the round

Of coming years, this board of ours

I hope may blossom and abound

.

" With shining curls, and laughing eyes,

And pleasant jests and merry words,

And questions full of life's surprise,

And light and music, when the birds

Have left us to our gloomy skies.

—" Now mount with me the old oak stair !

This is your chamber—pink and blue !

They asked the color of your hair,

And draped and fitted all for you,

My fine brunette, with tasteful care.

" The linen is as white as snow ;

The flowers are set on every sconce ;

And e'en the cushioned pin-heads show

Your formal " welcome " for the nonce,

To the sweet home their hands bestow.

" Declining to the river's marge,

See, from this window, how the turf

Runs with a thousand flowers in charge

To meet the silver feet of surf

That fly from every passing barge !

" Along that reach of liquid light

Flies Commerce with her countless keels ;

There the chained Titan in his might

Turns slowly round the groaning wheels

That drag her burdens, day and night.

" And now the red sun flings his kiss

Across its waves from finger-tips

That pause, and grudgingly dismiss

The one he loves to closer lips,

And Moonlight's quiet hour of bliss.

" And here comes Dinah with the steam,

Of evening cups and evening food,

And burning berries quenched with cream,

And ministry of homely good

That proves, my dear, we do not dream."

III.

He heard the long-drawn organ-peal

Within his chapel call to prayer;

And, answering with ready zeal,

He breathed o'er Mildred's weary chair

These words, and sealed them with a seal :

"Only a little hour I take ;—
But know that I am wholly yours,
And that a thousand bosoms ache
To tell you, that while life endures,
You shall be cherished for my sake.

"So throw your heart's door open wide,
And take in mine as well as me ;
Let no poor creature be denied
The grace of tender courtesy
And kindness from the pastor's bride."

IV.

The moon came up the summer sky :
"Oh, happy moon !" the lady said ;
"Men love thee for thyself, but I
Am loved because my life is wed
To one whose message, pure and high,

" Has spread the world's evangel far,

And thrown such radiance through the dark

That men behold him as a star,

And in his gracious coming mark

How beautiful his footsteps are.

" Oh, Moon! dost thou take all thy light

From the great sun so lately gone ?

Are there not shapes upon thy white,

That mould and make his sheen thy own,

And charms that soften to the sight

" The ardor of his blinding blaze ?

Who loves thee that thou art the sun's ?

Who does not give thee sweetest praise

Among the troop of shining ones

That sweep along the heavenly ways ?

"Yet still within the holy place

The altar sanctifies the gift !

Poor, precious gift, that begs for grace !

Oh, towering altar ! that doth lift

The gift so high, that, in its face,

"It bears no beauty to the thought

Of those who round the altar stand !

Poor, precious gift, that goes for naught

From willing heart and ready hand,

And wins no favor unbesought !

"The stars are whiter for the blue ;

The sky is deeper for the stars ;

They give and take in commerce true,

And lend their beauty to the cars

Of downy dusk, that all night through

"Sweep o'er the void on silver wheels;

Yet neither starry sky nor cloud

Is loved the less that it reveals

A beauty all its own, endowed

By all the wealth its beauty steals.

"Am I a dew-drop in a rose,

With no significance apart?

Must I but sparkle in repose

Close to its folded, fragrant heart,

Its peerless beauty to disclose?

"Would I not toil to win his bread,

Or give him all I have to give?

Would I not die in his sweet stead,

And die in joy? But I must live;

And, living, I must still be fed

" On love that comes in love's own right.

They must not pet or pamper me—

These who rejoice beneath his light—

Or pity him, that I can be

So precious in his princely sight."

With swiftest wings, through heart and brain,

The little hour unheeded flew ;

And when, behind the blazoned stain

Of saintly vestures, red and blue,

The lights on rose and window-pane

Within the chapel slowly died,

And figures muffled by the moon

Went shuffling home on either side—

One seeking her—she said : " How soon ! "

And the glad pastor kissed his bride.

V.

The bright night brightened into dawn ;

The shadows down the mountain passed ;

And tree and shrub and sloping lawn,

With bending, beaded beauty glassed

In myriad suns the sun that shone !

The robin fed her nested young ;

The swallows bickered 'neath the eaves ;

The hang-bird in her hammock swung,

And, tilting high among the leaves,

Her red mate sang alone, or flung

The dew-drops on her lifted head ;

While on the grasses, white and far,

The tents of fairy hosts were spread

That, scared before the morning star,

Had left their reeking camp, and fled.

The pigeon preened his opal breast ;

And o'er the meads the bobolink,

With vexed perplexity confessed

His tinkling gutturals in a kink,

Or giggled round his secret nest.

With dizzy wings and dainty craft,

In green and gold, the humming bird

Dashed here and there, and touched and quaffed

The honey-dew, then flashed and whirred,

And vanished like the feathered shaft

That glitters from a random bow.

The flies were buzzing in the sun,

The bees were busy in the snow

Of lilies, and the spider spun,

And waited for his prey below.

With sail aloft and sail adown,

And motion neither slow nor swift,

With dark-brown hull and shadow brown,

Half-way between two skies adrift,

The barque went dreaming toward the town.

'Twas Sunday in the silent street,

And Sunday in the silent sky.

The peace of God came down to meet

The throng that laid their labor by,

And rested weary hands and feet.

Ah, sweet the scene which caught the glance

Of eyes that with the morning woke,

And, from their window in the manse,

Looked up through sprays of elm and oak

Into the sky's serene expanse,

And off upon the distant wood,

And down into the garden's close,

And over, where his chapel stood

In ivy, reaching to its rose,

Waiting the Sunday multitude!

VI.

A red rose in her raven hair

Whose curls were held by plait and braid,

The bride swept down the oaken stair,

And mantled like a bashful maid,

As, seated in the waiting chair,

Behind the fragrant urn, she poured

The nectar of the morn's repast ;

But fairer lady, fonder lord,

In happier hall ne'er broke their fast

With sweeter bread, at prouder board.

And then they rose with common will,

And sought the parlor, cool and dim.

"Sing, love!" he said. "The birds grow still,

And wait with me to hear your hymn."

She swept a low, preluding thrill—

A spray of sound—across the keys

That felt her fingers for the first;

And then, from simplest cadences,

A reverent melody she nursed,

And gave it voice in words like these:

"From full forgetfulness of pain,

From joy to opening joy again,

With bird and flower, and hill and tree,

We lift our eyes and hands to thee,

To greet thee, Father, Lord of Heaven and Earth!

" That thou dost bathe our souls anew

With balm of light and heavenly dew,

And smilest in our upward eyes

From the far blue of smiling skies,

We bless thee, Father, Lord of Heaven and Earth:

" For human love and love divine,

For love of ours and love of thine,

For heaven on earth and heaven above—

To thee and us twin homes of love—

We thank thee, Father, Lord of Heaven and Earth!

" O dove-like wings, so wide unfurled

In brooding calm above the world !

Waft us your holy peace, and raise

The incense of our morning praise

Up to our Father, Lord of Heaven and Earth !"

VII.

Full fleetly sped the morning hours;

Then, wide upon the country round

A tumult of melodious powers

In tumult of melodious sound

Burst forth from all the village towers.

With blow on blow, and tone on tone,

And echoes answering everywhere—

Like bugles from the mountains blown—

Each sought to whelm the burdened air,

And make the silence all its own.

In broad, sonorous, silver swells

The air was billowed like the sea;

And listening ears were listening shells

That caught the Sabbath minstrelsy,

And sang it with the singing bells.

2

The billows heaved, the billows broke,

The first wild burst went down amain;

The music fell to slower stroke,

And in a rhythmic, bold refrain

The great bells to each other spoke.

Oh, bravely bronze gave forth his word,

And sharply silver made reply,

And every tower and turret stirred

With sounding breath and converse high,

Or paused with waiting ear and heard.

And long they talked, as friend to friend;

Then faltered to their closing toll,

Whose long, monotonous repetend,

From every music-burdened bowl

Poured the last drop, and brought the end!

VIII.

The chapel's chime fell slow and soft

And throngs slow-marching to its knoll

From village home and distant croft,

With careful feet and reverent soul

Pressed toward the open door, but oft

Turned curious and expectant eyes

Upon the Manse that stood apart.

There in her quiet, bridal guise

Fair Mildred sat with shrinking heart;

While Philip, bold and over-wise,

And knowing naught of woman's ways,

Smiled at her fears, and could not guess

How one so armored in his praise,

And strong in native loveliness,

Could dread to meet his people's gaze.

He could not know her fine alarm

When at his manly side she stood,

And, leaning faintly on his arm—

A dainty slip of womanhood—

Walked forth where every girlish charm

Was scanned with prying gaze and glance,

Among the slowly moving crowd

That, greedy of the precious chance,

Read furtively, but half aloud,

The pages of their new romance.

"A child!"   And Mildred caught the word.

"A plaything!"   And another voice :

"Fine feathers, and a Southern bird!"

And still one more :   "A parson's choice!"

And trembling Mildred overheard.

These from the careless or the dull—

These from the gossips and the dolts—

And though her quickened ear might cull

From out their whispered thunderbolts

A "lovely!" and a "beautiful!"

And though sweet mother-faces smiled,

And bows were given with friendly grace,

And many a pleasant little child

Sought sympathy within her face,

Her aching heart was not beguiled.

She did not see—she only felt—

As up the staring aisle she walked—

The critic glances, coldly dealt

By those who looked, and bent, and talked:

And, even, when at last she knelt

Alone within the pastor's pew,

And prayed for self-forgetfulness

With deep humility, she knew

She gave her figure and her dress

To careful eyes with closer view.

IX.

At length she raised her head, and tossed

A burden from her heart and brain.

She would have love at any cost

Of weary toil and patient pain,

Of rightful ease and pleasure lost!

They could not love her for his sake ;

They would not, and her heart forgave.

Why should a woman stoop to take

The poor endowment of a slave,

And, like a menial, choose to make

Her master's mantle half her own?

They loved her least who loved him most!

They envied her her little throne!

He who was cherished by a host

Was hers by gift, and hers alone;

And she would prove her woman's right

To hold the throne to which the king

Had called her, clothing her with white;

And never would she show her ring

To win a loving proselyte!

These were the thoughts and this the strife

That through her kindling spirit swept,

And wrought her purposes of life;

While powers that waked and powers that slept

Within the sweet and girlish wife,

Sprang into energy intense,

At touch of an inspiring chrism

That fell on her, she knew not whence,

And lifted her to heroism

Which wrapped her wholly, soul and sense.

X.

Meanwhile, through all the vaulted space

The organ sent its angels out ;

And up and down the holy place

They fanned the cheeks of care and doubt,

And touched each worn and weary face

With beauty as their wings went by :

Then sailed afar with peaceful sweep,

And, calling heavenward every eye,

Evanished into silence deep—

The earth forgotten in the sky !

Then by the sunlight warmly kissed,

Far up, in rainbow glory set,

Rayed round with gold and amethyst,

She saw upon the great rosette

The Saviour's visage, pale and trist.

" Oh, Crown of Thorns ! " she softly breathed ;

" Oh, precious crown of love divine !

Oh, brow with trickling life enwreathed !

Oh, piercing thorns and crimson sign !

I hold you mine in love bequeathed.

" But not for sake of these or thee !

I must win love as thou hast won.

The thorns are mine, and all must see,

In sacrifice, and service done,

The loving Lord they love in me."

2*

XI.

Then, through a large and golden hour

She listened to the golden speech

Of one who held the priceless dower

Of love and eloquence, that reach

And move the hearts of men with power.

Ah! poor the music of the choir

That voiced the Psalter after him!

And strong the prayer that, touched with fire,

Flamed upward, past the seraphim,

And wrapped the throne of his desire!

She watched and heard as in a dream,

When, in the old, familiar ground

Of sacred truth, he found his theme,

And led it forth, until it wound

Through meadows broad—a swollen stream

That flashed and eddied in the light,

And fed the grasses at its edge,

Or thundered in its onward might

O'er interposing weir and ledge,

And left them hidden in the white;

Then pressing onward to the eye,

Grew broader, till its breadth became

A solemn river, sweeping by,

That, quick with ships and red with flame,

Reached far away and kissed the sky!

Strong men were moved as trees are bowed

Before a swift and sounding wind;

And sighs were long and sobs were loud,

From loving saints and those who sinned,

Among the deeply listening crowd.

XII.

And Mildred, in the whelming tide

Of thought and feeling, quite forgot

That he who thus had magnified

His office, held a common lot

With her, and owned her as his bride.

But when, at length, the thought returned

That she was his in plighted truth,

And she with humbled soul discerned

That, though her youth was given to youth,

And love by love was fairly earned,

She could not match him, wing-and-wing,

Through all his broad and lofty range,

And thought what passing years might bring—

No change for good, but only change

That would degrade her to a thing

Of homely use and household care,

And love by duty basely kept—

She bowed her head upon the bare

Cold rail that hid her face, and wept,

And poured her passion in a prayer.

XIII.

" Oh, Father, Father! " thus she prayed :

" Thou know'st the priceless boon I seek !

Before my life, abashed, dismayed,

I stand, with hopeless hands and weak,

Of him and of myself afraid !

"'Teach me and lead me where to find,

Beyond the touch of hand and lip,

That vital charm of heart and mind

Which, in a true companionship,

My feebler life to his shall bind !

"His ladder leans upon the sun ;

I cannot climb it : give me wings !

Grant that my deeds, divinely done,

May be appraised divinest things,

Though they be little, every one.

    .

"His stride is strong ; his steps are high :

May not my deeds be little stairs

That, counted swift, shall keep me nigh,

Till at the summit, unawares,

We stand with equal foot and eye ?

"If further down toward Nature's heart

His root is struck, commanding springs

In whose deep life I have no part,

Send me, on recompensing wings,

The rain that gathers where thou art !

"Oh, give me vision to divine

What he with delving hand explores!

Feed me with flame that shall refine

To finest gold the rugged ores

His strong hands gather from the mine!

"So, dearest Father, shall no sloth,

Or weakness of my weaker soul,

Delay him in his kingly growth,

Or hold him meanly from the goal

That shines with guerdon for us both."

XIV.

Then all arose as if a spell

Had been dissolved for their release,

The while the benediction fell

Which breathed the gentle Master's peace

On all the souls that loved him well.

And Philip, coming from his place,

Like Moses from the mountain pyre,

Bore on his brow the shining grace

Of one who, in the cloud and fire,

Had met his Maker, face to face.

And men and women, young and old,

Pressed up to meet him as he came,

And children, by their love made bold,

Grasped both his hands and spoke his name,

And in their simple language told

Their joy to see his face once more;

While half in pleasure, half in pain,

His bride stood waiting at her door

The passage of the friendly train

That slowly swept the crowded floor.

Half-bows were tendered and returned;
And welcomes fell from lips and eyes;
But in her heart she meekly spurned
The love that came in love's disguise
Of sympathy—the love unearned.

XV.

Then out beneath the noon-day sun
Of the old Temple, cool and dim,
She walked beside her chosen one,
And lost her loneliness in him;
But hardly was her walk begun

When, straight before her in the street,
With tender shock her eye descried
A little child, with naked feet
And scanty dress, that, hollow-eyed,
Looked up and begged for bread to eat.

Nor haughty pride nor dainty spleen
Felt with her heart the sickening shock.
She took the hand so soiled and lean ;
And silken robe and ragged frock
Moved side by side across the green.

She looked for love, and, low and wild,
She found it—looking, too, for love !
So in each other's eyes they smiled,
As, dark brown hand in snowy glove,
The bride led home the hungry child.

And men and women in amaze
Paused in their homeward steps to see
The bride retreating from their gaze,
Clasped hand in hand with misery ;
Then brushed their eyes, and went their ways.

XVI.

When the long parley found a close,
And, clean and kempt, the little oaf—
Disburdened of her wants and woes,
And loaded with her wheaten loaf—
Went forth to minister to those

Who sent her on her bitter quest,
The bride stood smiling at her door,
And in her happiness confessed
That she had found a friend ; nay, more—
Had entertained a heavenly guest.

And as she watched her down the street,
Her brow grown bright with sunny thought,
Her heart o'erfilled with something sweet,
She knew the vagrant child had brought
The blessing of the Paraclete.

She turned from out the blazing noon,

And sought her chamber's quiet shade,

Like one who had received a boon

She might not show, but which essayed

Expression in a happy croon.

And then, outleaping from the mesh

Of Memory's net, like bird or bee,

There thrilled her spirit and her flesh

This old half-song, half-rhapsody,

That sang, or said itself, afresh :

"Poor little wafer of silver!

More precious to me than its cost!

It was worn of both image and legend,

But priceless because it was lost.

My chamber I carefully swept;

I hunted, and wondered, and wept;

And I found it at last with a cry :

Oh, dear little treasure ! said I ;

And I washed it with tears all the day :

Then I kissed it, and put it away.

" Poor little lamb of the sheepfold !

Unlovely and feeble it grew ;

But it wandered away to the mountains,

And was fairer the further it flew.

I followed with hurrying feet

At the call of its pitiful bleat,

And precious, with wonderful charms,

I caught it at last in my arms,

And bore it far back to its keep,

And kissed it and put it to sleep.

" Poor little vagrant from Heaven !

It wandered away from the fold,

And its weakness and danger endowed it

With value more precious than gold.

Oh, happy the day when it came,

And my heart learned its beautiful name!

Oh, happy the hour when I fed

This waif of the angels with bread!

And the lamb that the Shepherd had missed

Was sheltered and nourished and kissed!"

XVII.

To Philip, Mildred was a child,

Or a fair angel, to be kept

From all things earthly undefiled,—

Who on his loving bosom slept,

And only waked to be beguiled

From loneliness and homely care

By love's unfailing ministry.

No toil of his was she to share,

No burden hers, that should not be

Left for his stronger hands to bear.

His love enwrapped her as a robe,

Which seemed, by its supernal charm,

To shield from every poisoned probe

Of earthly pain and earthly harm

This one choice creature of the globe.

The love he bore her lifted him

Into a bright, sweet atmosphere

That filled with beauty to the brim

The world beneath him, far and near,

And stained the clouds that draped its rim.

Toil was not toil, except in name ;

Care was not care, but only means

To feed with holy oil the flame

That warmed her soul, and lit the scenes

Through which her figure went and came.

Her smile of welcome was his meed;

Her presence was his great reward;

He questioned sadly if, indeed,   .

He loved more loyally his Lord,

Or if his Lord felt greater need.

And Mildred, vexed, misunderstood,

Knew all his love, but might not tell

How in his thought, so large and good,

And in his heart, there did not dwell

The measure of her womanhood.

She knew the girlish charm would fade;

She knew the rapture would abate;

That years would follow when the maid,

Merged in the matron, and sedate

With change, and sitting in the shade

Of a great nature, would become

As poor and pitiful a thing

As an old idol, and as dumb,—

A clog upon an upward wing,—

A value stricken from the sum

Which a true woman's hand would raise

To mighty numbers, and endow

With kingly power and crowning praise.

She must be mate of his; but how?

And, dreaming of a thousand ways

Her hands would work, her feet would tread,

She thought to match him as a man!

His books should be her daily bread;

She would run swiftly where he ran,

And follow closely where he led.

3

XVIII.

Since time began, the perfect day
Has robbed the morrow of its wealth,
And squandered, in its lavish sway,
The balm and beauty of the stealth,
And left its golden throne in gray.

So when the Sunday light declined,
A cold wind sprang and shut the flowers :
Then vagrant voices, undefined,
Grew louder through the evening hours,
Till the old chimney howled and whined

As if it were a frightened beast,
That witnessed from its dizzy post
The loathsome forms and grewsome feast
And hideous mirth of ghoul and ghost,
As on they crowded from the East.

The willow, gathered into sheaves

Of scorpions by spectral arms,

Swung to and fro, and whipped the eaves,

And filled the house with weird alarms

That hissed from all its tortured leaves.

And in the midnight came the rain ;—

In spiteful needles at the first ;

But soon on roof and window-pane

The slowly gathered fury burst

In floods that came, and came again,

And poured their roaring burden out.

They swept along the sounding street,

Then paused, and then with shriek and shout

Hurtled as if a myriad feet

Had joined the dread and deafening rout.

But ere the welcome morning broke,

The loud wind fell, though gray and chill

The drizzling rain and drifting smoke

Drove slowly toward the westward hill,

Half hidden in its phantom cloak.

And through the mist a clumsy smack,

Deep loaded with her clumsy freight,

With shifting boom and frequent tack,

Like a huge ghost that wandered late,

Reeled by upon her devious track.

XIX.

So Mildred, with prophetic ken,

Saw in the long and rainy day

The dreaded host of friendly men

And friendly women, kept away,

And time for love, and book, and pen.

But while she looked, with dreaming eyes

And heart content, upon the scene,

She saw a stalwart man arise

Where the wild water lashed the green,

And pause a breath, to signalize

Some one beyond her stinted view;

Then turn with hurried feet, and straight

The deep, rain-burdened grasses through,

And through the manse's open gate,

Pass to her door. At once she knew

That some faint soul, in sad extreme,

Had sent for succor to the manse,

And knew its master would redeem

To sacred use the circumstance

That made such havoc of her scheme.

XX.

She saw the quiet men depart,

She saw them leave the river-side,

She saw them brave with sturdy art

The surges of the angry tide,

And disappear ; the while her heart

Sank down in dismal loneliness.

Then came her vexing thoughts again ;

And quick, as if she broke duress

Of heavy weariness or pain,

She sought the study's dim recess,

Where rank on rank, against the wall,

The mighty men of every land

Stood mutely waiting for the call

Of him who, with his single hand,

Had bravely met and mastered all.

The gray old monarchs of the pen

Looked down with calm, benignant gaze,

And Augustine and Origen

And Ansel justified the ways—

The wondrous ways—of God with men.

Among the tall hierophants

Angelical Aquinas stood ;

While Witsius held the " Covenants,"

And Irenæus, wise and good,

Couched low his silver-bearded lance

For strife with heresy and schism,

And Turretin with lordly nod

Gave system to the dogmatism

That analyzed the thought of God

As light is painted by a prism.

Great Luther, with his great disputes,

And Calvin, with his finished scheme,

And Charnock, with his " Attributes,"

And Taylor with his poet's dream

Of theologic flowers and flutes,

And Thomas Fuller, old and quaint,

And Cudworth, dry with dust of gold,

And South, the sharp and witty saint,

With Howe and Owen—broad and bold—

And Leighton still without the taint

Of earth upon his robe of white,

Stood side by side with Hobbes and Locke,

And—braced by many an acolyte—

With Edwards standing on his rock,

And all New England's men of might,

Whose gifts and offices divine

Had crowned her with a kingly crown,

And solemn doctors from the Rhine,

With Fichte, Kant, and Hegel, down

Through all the long and stately line!

As Mildred saw the awful host,

She felt within no motive stir

To realize her girlish boast,

And knew they held no more for her

Than if each volume were a ghost.

XXI.

She sat in Philip's vacant chair,

And pondered long her doubtful way ;

And, in her impotent despair,

Lifted her longing eyes to pray,

When on a shelf, far up and bare,

She saw an ancient volume lie ;

And straight her rising thought was checked.

What were its dubious treasures?   Why

Had it been banished from respect,

And from its owner's hand and eye?

The more she gazed, the stronger grew

The wish to hold it in her hand.

Strange fancies round the volume flew,

And changed the dust their pinions fanned

To atmospheres of red and blue,

That blent in purple aureole,—

As if a lymph of sweetest life

Stood warm within a golden bowl,

Crowned with its odor-cloud, and rife

With strength and solace for her soul!

And there it lay beyond her arm,

And wrought its fine and wondrous spell,

With all its hoard of good or harm,

Till curious Mildred, struggling well,

Surrendered to the mighty charm :

The steps were scaled for boon or bale,

The book was lifted from its place,

And, bowing to the fragrant grail,

She drank with pleased and eager face

This draught from off an Eastern tale :

SELIM AND NOURMAHAL.

Selim, the haughty Jehangir, the Conquerer of the
Earth,

With royal pomps and pageantries and rites of festal
mirth

Was set to celebrate the day—the white day—of his
birth.

His red pavilions, stretching wide, crowned all with
globes of gold,

And tipped with pinnacles of fire and streamers mani-
fold,

Flamed with such splendor that the sun at noon
looked pale and cold!

And right and left, along the plain, far as the eye
could gaze,

His nobles and retainers who were tented in the
blaze,

Kept revel high in honor of that day of all the
days.

The earth was spread, the walls were hung, with
silken fabrics fine,

And arabesque and lotus-flower bore each the broid-
ered sign

Of jewels plucked from land and sea, and red gold
from the mine.

Upon his throne he sat alone, half buried in the
gems

That strewed his tapestries like stars, and tipped
their tawny hems,

And glittered with the glory of a hundred dia-
dems.

He saw from his pavilion door the nodding heron-
    plumes
His nobles wore upon their brows, while, from the
    rosy glooms
Which hid his harem, came low songs, on wings of
    rare perfumes!

The elephants, a thousand strong, had passed his
    dreaming eye,
Caparisoned with golden plates on head and breast
    and thigh,
And a hundred flashing troops of horse unmarked had
    thundered by.

He sat upon old Akbar's throne, the heir of power
    and fame;
But all his glory was as dust, and dust his wondrous
    name—
Swept into air, and scattered far, by one consuming
    flame!

For on that day of all the days, and in that festal
  hour,
He sickened with his glory and grew weary of his
  power,
And pined to bind upon his breast his harem's choi-
  cest flower.

" Oh Nourmahal! oh Nourmahal! why sit I here," he
  cried,—
" The victim of these gaudy shows, and of my haughty
  pride,
When thou art dearer to my soul than all the world
  beside !

" Thy eyes are brighter than the gems piled round
  my gilded seat ;
Thy cheeks are softer than the silks that shimmer at
  my feet,
And purer heart than thine in woman's breast hath
  never beat!

"My first love—and my only love—Oh babe of Can-
    dahar!

Torn from my boyish arms at first, and, like a silver
    star

Shining within another heaven, and worshipped from
    afar,

"Thou art my own at last, my own! I pine to see
    thy face;

Come to me, Nourmahal! Oh come, and hallow with
    thy grace

The glories that without thy love are meaningless and
    base!"

He spoke a word, and, quick as light, before him,
    lying prone

A dark-eyed page, with gilded vest and crimson-belted
    zone,

Looked up with waiting ear to mark the message from
    the throne.

"Go summon Nourmahal, my queen; and when her
  radiance comes,

Bear my command of silence to the vinas and the
  drums,

And for your guerdon take your choice of all these
  gilded crumbs."

He tossed a handful of the gems down where his
  minion lay,

Who snatched a jewel from the drift, and swiftly sped
  away

With his command to Nourmahal, who waited to
  obey.

.

But needlessly the mandate fell of silence on the
  crowd,

For when the Empress swept the path, ten thousand
  heads were bowed,

And drum and vina ceased their din, and no one
  spoke aloud.

As comes the moon from out the sea with her attend-
    ant breeze,
As sweeps the morning up the hills and blossoms in
    the trees,
So Nourmahal to Selim came : then fell upon her
    knees !

The envious jewels looked at her with chill, barbaric
    stare,
The cloth-of-gold she knelt upon grew lustreless and
    bare,
And all the place was cooler in the darkness of her
    hair.

And while she knelt in queenly pride and beauty
    strange and wild,
And held her breast with both her palms and looked
    on him and smiled,
She seemed no more of common earth, but Casyapa's
    child.

He bent to her as thus she smiled; he kissed her
lifted cheek;

" Oh Nourmahal," he murmured low, " more dear
than I can speak,

I'm weary of my lonely life : give me the rest I
seek."

She rose and paced the silken floor, as if in mad ca-
price,

Then paused, and from the Empress changed to im-
provisatrice,

And wove this song—a golden chain—that led him
into peace :

" Lovely children of the light,
Draped in radiant locks and pinions,—
Red and purple, blue and white
In their beautiful dominions,
On the earth and in the spheres,
Dwell the little glendoveers.

" And the red can know no change,

And the blue are blue forever,

And the yellow wings may range

Toward the white or purple never.

But they mingle free from strife,

For their color is their life.

" When their color dies, they die,—

Blent with earth or ether slowly—

Leaving where their spirits lie,

Not a stain, so pure and holy

Is the essence and the thought

Which their fading brings to naught !

" Each contented with the hue

Which indues his wings of beauty,

Red or yellow, white or blue,

Sings the measure of his duty

Through the summer clouds in peace,

And delights that never cease.

" Not with envy love they more

Locks and pinions purple-tinted,

Nor with jealousy adore

Those whose pleasures are unstinted

And whose purple hair and wings

Give them place with queens and kings.

" When a purple glendoveer

Flits along the mute expanses,

They surround him, far and near,

With their glancing wings and dances,

And do honor to the hue

Loved by all and worn by few.

" In the days long gone, alas !

Two upon a cloud, low-seated,

Saw their pinions in the glass

Of a silver lake repeated.

One was blue and one was red,

And the lovely pair were wed.

" ' Purple wings are very fine,'
  Spoke the voice of Ruby, gently :
  ' Ay,' said Sapphire, ' they're divine !'—
  Looking at his blue intently.
  ' But to wish for change is vain,'
  Ruby said : ' We'll not complain.'

" Sapphire stretched his loving arms,
  And she nestled on his bosom,
  While his heart inhaled her charms
  As the sense inhales a blossom ;—
  Drank her wholly, tint and tone,
  Blent her being with his own.

" Rapture passed, they raised their eyes,
  But were startled into clamor
  Of a marvellous surprise !
  Was it color ! was it glamour !
  Purple-tinted, sweet and warm,
  Was each wing and folded form !

" Who had wrought it—how it came—
These were what the twain disputed.
How were mingled smoke and flame
Into royal hue transmuted ?
Each was right, and each was wrong ;
But their quarrel was not long,

" For the moment that their speech
Differed o'er their little story,
Swiftly faded off from each
Every trace of purple glory ;
Blue was bluer than before,
And the red was red once more.

" Then they knew that both were wrong,
And in sympathy of sorrow
Learned that each was only strong
In the power to lend and borrow,—
That the purple never grew
But by grace of red to blue.

" So, embracing in content,
　　Hearts and wings again united,
　　Red and blue in purple blent,
　　And their holy troth replighted,
　　Both, as happy as the day,
　　Kissed, and rose, and flew away !

" And for twice a thousand years,
　　Floating through the radiant ether,
　　Lived the happy glendoveers,
　　Of the other, jealous neither,—
　　Sapphire naught without the red,
　　Ruby still by blue bested.

" Then when weary of their life,
　　They came down to earth at even—
　　Purple husband, purple wife—
　　From the upper deeps of heaven,
　　And reclined upon the grass,
　　That their little lives might pass.

" Wing to wing and arms enwreathed,

Sinking from their life's long dreaming

Into earth their souls they breathed ;

But when morning's light was streaming,

All their joys and sweet regrets

Bloomed in banks of violets ! "

As from its dimpled fountain, at its own capricious
will,

Each step a note of music, and each fall and flash a
thrill,

The rill goes singing to the meadow levels and is
still,

So fell from Nourmahal her song upon the captive
sense ;

It dashed in spray against the throne, it tinkled through
the tents,

And died at last among the flowery banks of recompense ;

4

For when great Selim marked her fire, and read her
  riddle well,
And watched her from the flushing to the fading of
  the spell,
He sprang forgetful from his seat, and caught her as
  she fell.

He raised her in his tender arms; he bore her to his
  throne:
"No more, oh! Nourmahal, my wife, no more I sit
  alone;
And the future for the dreary past shall royally
  atone!"

He called to him the princes and the nobles of the
  land,
Then took the signet-ring from his, and placed it on
  her hand,
And bade them honor as his own, fair Nourmahal's
  command.

And on the minted silver that his largess scattered
   wide,

And on the gold of commerce, till the mighty Selim
   died,

Her name and his in shining boss stood equal, side
   by side.

XXII.

The opening of the wondrous tome

Was like the opening of a door

Into a vast and pictured dome,

Crowded, from vaulted roof to floor,

With secrets of her life and home.

To be like Philip was to be

Another Philip—only less!

To win his wit in full degree

Would bear to him but nothingness,

From one no wiser grown than he!

If blue and red in Hindostan

At home were also red and blue,

She learned that woman and that man

Had never worn the royal hue

Till blue and red together ran

In complement of each to each;

She might not tint his life at all

By learning wisdom he could teach;

So what she gave, though poor and small,

Should be of that beyond his reach.

Where Philip fed, she would not feed;

Where Philip walked, she would not go;

The books he read she would not read,

But live her separate life, and, so,

Have sole supplies to meet his need.

He held his mission and his range;

His way and work were all his own;

And she would give him in exchange

What she could win and she alone,

Of life and learning, fresh and strange.

XXIII.

While thus she sat in musing mood,

Determining her life's emprise,

The sunlight flushed the distant wood,

Then, coming closer, filled her eyes,

And glorified her solitude.

The clouds were shivered by the lance

Sped downward by the morning sun,

And from her heart, in swift advance,

The shadows vanished, one by one,

Till more than sunlight filled the manse.

She closed the volume with a gust

That sprent the light with powdered gold;

Then placed it high to hide and rust

Where, curious and over bold

She found it, lying in its dust.

Her soul was light, her path was plain;

One shadow only drooped above,—

The shadow of a heart and brain

So charged with overwhelming love

That it oppressed and gave her pain.

The modest comb that kept her hair;

To Philip was a golden crown;

And every ringlet was a snare,

And every hat, and every gown

And slipper, something more than fair.

His love had glorified her grace,

And she was his, and not her own,—

So wholly his she had no place

Beside him on his lonely throne,

Or share in love's divine embrace.

But still she saw and held her plan,

And fear made way for springing hope.

If she was man's, then hers was man :

Both held their own in even scope ;

And then and there her life began.

LOVE'S PHILOSOPHIES.

I.

A WIFE is like an unknown sea ;—
Least known to him who thinks he knows
Where all the Shores of Promise be,
Where lie the Islands of Repose,
And where the rocks that he must flee.

Capricious winds, uncertain tides,
Drive the young sailor on and on,
Till all his charts and all his guides
Prove false, and vain conceit is gone,
And only docile Love abides.

Where lay the shallows of the maid,

No plummet-line the wife may sound;

Where round the sunny islands played

The pulses of the great profound,

Lies low the treacherous everglade.

And, as he sails, he is, perforce,

Discoverer of a strange new world;

And finds, whate'er may be his course,

Green lands within white seas impearled,

With streams of unsuspected source

Which feed with gold delicious fruits,

Kept by unguessed Hesperides,

Or cool the lips of gentle brutes

That breed and browse among the trees

Whose wind-tossed limbs and leaves are lutes.

4*

The maiden free, the maiden wed,

Can never, never be the same.

A new life springs from out the dead,

And, with the speaking of a name,

A breath upon the marriage-bed,

She finds herself a something new—

(Which he learns later, but no less) ;

And good and evil, false and true,

May change their features—who can guess?—

Seen close, or from another view.

For maiden life, with all its fire,

Is hid within a grated cell,

Where every fancy and desire

And graceless passion, guarded well,

Sits dumb behind the woven wire.

Marriage is freedom : only when

The husband turns the prison-key

Knows she herself ; nor even then

Knows she more wisely well than he

Who finds himself least wise of men.

New duties bring new powers to birth,

And new relations, new surprise

Of depths of weakness or of worth,

Until he doubt if her disguise

Mask more of heaven, or more of earth.

Tears spring beneath a careless touch ;

Endurance hardens with a word ;

She holds a trifle with a clutch

So strangely, childishly absurd,

That he who loves and pardons much

Doubts if her wayward wit be sane,

When straight beyond his manly power

She stiffens to the awful strain

Of some supreme or crucial hour,

And stands unblanched in fiercest pain!

A jealous thought, a petty pique,

Enwraps in gloom, or bursts in storm ;

She questions all that love may speak,

And weighs its tone, and marks its form,

Or yields her frailty to a freak

That vexes him or breeds disgust ;

Then rises in heroic flame,

And treads a danger into dust,

Or puts his doubting soul to shame

With love unfeigned and perfect trust.

Still seas unknown the husband sails;

Life-long the lovely marvel lasts;

In golden calms or driving gales,

With silent prow or reeling masts,

Each hour a fresh surprise unveils.

The brooding, threatening bank of mist

Grows into groups of virid isles,

By sea embraced and sunlight kissed,

Or breaks into resplendent smiles

Of cinnabar and amethyst!

No day so bright but scuds may fall,

No day so still but winds may blow;

No morn so dismal with the pall

Of wintry storm, but stars may glow

When evening gathers, over all!

And so thought Philip, when, in haste

Returning from his lengthened stay—

The river and the lawn retraced—

He found his Mildred blithe and gay,

And all his anxious care a waste.

To be half vexed that she could thrive

Without him through a morning's span,

Upon the honey in her hive,

Was but to prove himself a man

And show that he was quite alive!

II.

A sympathetic word or kiss,

(Mildred had insight to discern,)

Though grateful quite, is quite amiss,

In leading to the life etern

The soul that has no bread in this.

The present want must aye be fed,

And first relieved the present care :

" Give us this day our daily bread "

Must be recited in our prayer

Before " forgive us " may be said.

And he who lifts a soul from vice,

And leads the way to better lands ;

Must part his raiment, share his slice,

And oft with weary, bleeding hands,

Pave the long path with sacrifice.

So on a pleasant summer morn,

Wrapped in her motive, sweet and safe,

She sought the homes of sin and scorn,

And found her little Sunday waif

Ragged, and hungry, and forlorn.

She called her quickly to her knee;

And with her came a motley troop

Of children, poor and foul as she,

Who gathered in a curious group,

And ceased their play, to hear and see.

Tanned brown by all the summer suns,

With brutish brows and vacant eyes,

They drank her speech and ate her buns,

While she behind their sad disguise

Beheld her dear Lord's "little ones."

She stood like Ruth amid the wheat,

With ready hand and sickle keen,

And looked on all with aspect sweet;

For where she only thought to glean,

She found a harvest round her feet.

Ah! little need the tale to write
Of garments begged from door to door,
Of needles plying in the night,
And money gathered from the store
Alike of screw and Sybarite,

With which to clothe the little flock.
She went like one sent forth of God
To loose the bolts of heart and lock,
And with the smiting of her rod
To call a flood from every rock.

And little need the tale to tell
How, when the Sunday came again,
A wondrous change the group befell,
And how from every noisome den,
Responding to the chapel bell,

They issued forth with shout and call,
And Mildred walking at their head,
Who, with her silken parasol,
Bannered the army that she led,
And with low words commanded all.

The little army walked through smiles
That hung like lamps above their march,
And lit their swart and straggling files,
While bending elm and plumy larch
Shaped into broad cathedral aisles

The paths that led with devious trend
To where the ivied chapel stood.
There their long passage found its end,
And there they gathered in a brood
Of gentle clamor round their friend.

A score pressed in on either side

To share the burden of her care,

And hearts and house gave entrance wide

To those to whom the words of prayer

Were stranger than the curse of pride.

And Mildred who, without a thought

Of glory in her week's long task,

This marvel of the week had wrought,

Had earned the boon she would not ask,

And won more love than she had sought.

III.

As two who walk through forest aisles,

Lit all the way by forest flowers,

Divide at morn through twin defiles

To meet again in distant hours,

With plunder plucked from all the miles,

So Philip and so Mildred went

Into their walks of daily life,—

Parting at morn with sweet consent,

And—tireless husband, busy wife—

Together when the day was spent,

Bringing the treasures they had won

From sundered tracks of enterprise,

To learn from each what each had done,

And prove each other grown more wise

Than when the morning was begun.

He strengthened her with manly thought

And learning, gathered from the great;

And she, whose quicker eye had caught

The treasures of the broad estate

Of common life and learning, brought

Her gleanings from the level field,

And gave them gladly to his hands,

Who had not dreamed that they could yield

Such sheaves, or hold within their bands

Such wealth of lovely flowers concealed.

His grave discourse, his judgment sure,

Gave tone and temper to her soul,

While her swift thoughts and vision pure,

And mirth that would not brook control,

And wit that kept him insecure

Within his dignified repose,

Refreshed and quickened him like wine.

No tender word or dainty gloze

Could give him pleasure half so fine

As that which tingled to her blows.

He gave her food for heart and mind,

And raised her toward his higher plane;

She showed him that his eyes were blind;

She proved his lofty wisdom vain,

And held him humbly with his kind.

IV.

Oh, blessed sleep! in which exempt

From our tired selves long hours we lie,

Our vapid worthlessness undreamt,

And our poor spirits saved thereby

From perishing of self-contempt!

We weary of our petty aims;

We sicken with our selfish deeds;

We shrink and shrivel in the flames

That low desire ignites and feeds,

And grudge the debt that duty claims.

Oh sweet forgetfulness of sleep !

Oh bliss, to drop the pride of dress,

And all the shams o'er which we weep,

And, toward our native nothingness,

To drop ten thousand fathoms deep !

At morning only—strong, erect—

We face our mirrors not ashamed ;

For then alone we meet unflecked

The image we at evening blamed,

And find refreshed our self-respect.

Ah ! little wonderment that those,

Who see us most and love us best,

Find that a true affection grows

More strong and sweet in tone and zest

Through frequent partings and repose.

Our fruit grows dead in pulp and rind

When seen and handled overmuch;

The roses fade, our fingers bind;

And with familiar kiss and touch

The graces wither from our kind.

Man lives on love, at love's expense,

And woman, so her love be sweet;

Best honey palls upon the sense

When it is tempted to repeat

Too oft its fine experience.

And Mildred, with instinctive skill,

And loving neither most nor least,

Stood out from Philip's grasping will,

And gave, where he desired a feast,

The taste that left him hungry still.

She hid her heart behind a mask,

And held him to his manly course ;

One hour in love she bade him bask,

And then she drove, with playful force,

The laggard to his daily task.

They went their way and kept their care,

And met again—their toil complete,—

Like angels on a heavenly stair,

Or pilgrims in a golden street,

Grown stronger one, and one more fair!

v.

As one worn down by petty pains,

With fevered head and restless limb,

Flies from the toil that stings and stains,

And all the cares that wearied him,

And some far, silent summit gains ;

5

And in its strong, sweet atmosphere,

Or in the blue, or in the green,

Finds his discomforts disappear,

And loses in the pure serene

The garnered humors of a year;

And sees not how and knows not when

The old vexations leave their seat,

So Philip, happiest of men,

Saw all his petty cares retreat,

And vanish, not to come again.

Where he had thought to shield and serve,

Himself had ministry instead;

He heard no vexing call to swerve

From larger toil, for labors sped

By Mildred's finer wit and nerve.

In deft and deferential ways
She took the house by silent siege ;
And Dinah, warmest in her praise,
Grew, unaware, her loyal liege,
And served her truly all her days.

And many a sad and stricken maid,
And many a lorn and widowed life
That came for counsel or for aid
To Philip, met the pastor's wife,
And on her heart their burden laid.

VI.

He gave her what she took—her will ;
And made it space for life full-orbed.
He learned at last that every rill
Loses its freshness, when absorbed
By the great stream that turns the mill.

With hand ungrasping for her dower,
He found its royal income his ;
And every swiftly kindling power—
Self-moved in its activities—
Becoming brighter every hour.

The air is sweet which we inspire
When it is free to come and go ;
And sound of brook and scent of brier
Rise freshest where the breezes blow,
That feed our breath and fan our fire.

That love is weak which is too strong;
A man may be a woman's grave ;
The right of love swells oft to wrong,
And silken bonds may bind a slave
As truly as a leathern thong.

We may not dine upon the bird

That fills our home with minstrelsy;

The living vine may never gird

Too firm and close the living tree,

Without sad sacrifice incurred.

The crystal goblet that we drain

Will be forever after dry;

But he who sips, and sips again,

And leaves it to the open sky,

Will find it filled with dew and rain.

The lilies burst, the roses blow

Into divinest balm and bloom,

When free above and free below;

And life and love must have large room,

That life and love may largest grow.

So Philip learned (what Mildred saw),

That love is like a well profound,

From which two souls have right to draw,

And in whose waters will be drowned

The one who takes the other's law.

VII.

Ambition was an alien word,

Which Mildred faintly understood;

Its poisoned breathing had not blurred

The whiteness of her womanhood,

Nor had its blatant trumpet stirred

To quicker pulse her heart content.

In social tasks and home employ,

She did not question what it meant;

But bore her woman's lot with joy

And sweetness, wheresoe'er she went.

If ever with unconscious thrill
It touched her, in some vagrant dream,
She only wished that God would fill
With larger tide the goodly stream
That flowed beside her, strong and still.

She knew that love was more than fame,
And happy conscience more than love ;—
Far off and wild, the wings of flame !
Close by, the pinions of the dove
That hovered white above her name !

She honored Philip as a man,
And joyed in his supreme estate ;
But never dreamed that under ban
She lives who never can be great,
Or chieftain of a crowd or clan.

The public eye was like a knife
That pierced and plagued her shrinking heart,
To be a woman, and a wife,
With privilege to dwell apart,
And hold unseen her modest life—

Alike from praise and blame aloof;
And free to live and move in peace
Beneath Love's consecrated roof—
Was boon so great she could not cease
Her thanks for the divine behoof.

Black turns to rust and blue to blight
Beneath the shining of the sun ;
And e'en the spotless robe of white,
Worn overlong, grows dim and dun
Through the strange alchemy of light.

Nor wife nor maiden, weak or brave,

Can stand and face the public stare,

And win the plaudits she may crave,

And stem the hisses she may dare,

And modest truth and beauty save.

No woman, in her soul, is she

Who longs to poise above the roar

Of motley multitudes, and be

The idol at whose feet they pour

The wine of their idolatry.

Coarse labor makes its doer coarse ;

Great burdens harden softest hands ;

A gentle voice grows harsh and hoarse

That warns and threatens and commands

Beyond the measure of its force.

5*

Oh sweet, beyond all speech, to feel

Within no answer to the drum,

Or echo to the bugle-peal,

That calls to duties which benumb

In service of the commonweal!

Oh sweet to feel, beyond all speech,

That most and best of human kind

Have leave to live beyond the reach

Of toil that tarnishes, and find

No tongue but Envy's to impeach!

Oh sweet, that most unnoticed deeds

Give play to fine, heroic blood!—

That hid from light, and shut from weeds,

The rose is fairer in its bud

Than in the blossom that succeeds!

He is the helpless slave who must;

And she enfranchised who may sit

Unblamed above the din and dust,

Where stronger hands and coarser wit

Strive equally for crown and crust.

So ran her thought, and broader yet,

Who scanned her own by Philip's pace;

And never did the wife forget

Her grateful tribute for the grace

That charged her with so sweet a debt.

So ran her thought; and in her breast

Her wifely pride to pity grew,

That Philip, by his Lord's behest—

To duty and to nature true—

Must do his bravest and his best,

Through winter's cold and summer's heat,

Where all might praise and all might blame,

And thus be topic of the street,

And see his fair and honest name

A football, kicked by careless feet.

Sho loved her creed, and doubting not

She read it well from Nature's scroll,

She found no line or word to blot;

But, from her woman's modest soul,

Thanked her Creator for her lot.

VIII.

He who, upon an Alpine peak,

Stands, when the sunrise lifts the East,

And gilds the crown and lights the cheek

Of largest monarch down to least,

Of all the summits cold and bleak,

Finds sadly that it brings no boon

For all his long and toilsome leagues,

And chill at once and weary soon,

Rests from his fevers and fatigues,

And waits the recompense of noon.

For then the valleys, near and far,

The hillsides, fretted by the vine,

The glacier-drift, the torrent-scar

Whose restless waters shoot and shine,

The silver tarn, that like a star

Trembles and flames with stress of light,

And scattered hamlet and chalet

That dot with brown, or paint with white,

The landscape quivering in the day,

With beauty all his toil requite.

Mountains, from mountain altitudes,

Are only hills, as bleak and bare ;

And he whose daring step intrudes

Upon their grandeur, and the rare

Cold light or gloom that o'er them broods,

Finds that with even brow to stand

Among the heights that bade him climb,

Is loss of all that made them grand,

While all of lovely and sublime

Looks up to him from lake and land.

Great men are few, and stand apart ;

And seem divinest when remote.

From brain to brain, and heart to heart,

No thoughts of genial commerce float :

Each holds his own exclusive mart.

And when we meet them, face to face,

And hand to hand their greatness greet,

Our steps we willingly retrace,

And gather humbly at their feet,

With those who live upon their grace.

And man and woman—mount and vale—

Have charms, each from the other seen,—

The robe of rose, the coat of mail :

The springing turf, the black ravine :

The tossing pines, the waving swale :

Which please the sight with constant joy.

Thus living, each has power to call

The other's thoughts with sweet decoy,

And one can rise and one can fall

But to distemper or destroy.

The dewy meadow breeds the cloud

That rises on ethereal wings,

And wraps the mountain in a shroud

From which the living lightning springs

And torrents pour, that, lithe and loud,

Leap down in service to the plains,

Or feed the fountains at their source;

And only thus the mountain gains

The vital fulness of the force

That fills the meadow's myriad veins.

In fair, reciprocal exchange

Of good which each appropriates,

The meadow and the mountain-range

Nourish their beautiful estates;

And lofty wild and lowly grange

Thrive on the commerce thus ordained ;

And not a reek ascends the rock,

And not a drift of dew is rained,

But eyrie-brood or tended flock

By the sweet gift is entertained.

A meadow may be fair and broad,

And hold a river in its rest ;

Or small, and with the silver gaud

Of a lone lakelet on its breast,

Or but a patch, that, overawed,

Clings humbly to the mountain's hem :

It matters not : it is the charm

That cheers his life, and holds the stem

Of every flower that tempts his arm,

Or greets his snowy diadem.

Dolts talk of largest and of least,

And worse than dolts are they who prate

Of Beauty captive to the Beast;

For man in woman finds his mate,

And thrones her equal at his feast.

She matches meekness with his might,

And patience with his power to act,—

His judgment with her quicker sight;

And wins by subtlety and tact

The battles he can only fight.

And she who strives to take the van

In conflict, or the common way,

Does outrage to the heavenly plan,

And outrage to the finer clay

That makes her beautiful to man.

All this, and more than this, she saw
Who reigned in Philip's house and heart.
Far off, he seemed without a flaw;
Close by, her tasteless counterpart,
And slave to Nature's common law.

To climb with fierce, familiar stride
His dizzy paths of life and thought,
Would but degrade him from her pride,
And bring the majesty to naught
Which love and distance magnified.

If she should grow like him, she knew
He would admire and love her less;
The eagle's image might be true,
But eagle of the wilderness
Would find no consort in the view.

A woman, in her woman's sphere,
A loyal wife and worshipper,
She only thirsted to appear
As fair to him as he to her,
And fairer still, from year to year.

And he who quickly learned to purge
His fancy of the tender whim
That she was floating at the verge
Of womanhood, half hid to him,
Saw her with gracious mien emerge,

And stand full-robed upon the shore,
With faculties and charms unguessed;
With wondrous eyes that looked before,
And hands that helped and words that blessed—
The mistress of an alien lore

Beyond the wisdom of the schools

And all his manly power to win;

With handicraft of tricks and tools

That conjured marvels with a pin,

And miracles with skeins and spools!

She seemed to mock his dusty dearth

With flowers that sprang beneath his eyes;

Till all he was, seemed little worth,

And she he deemed so little wise,

Became the wisest of the earth.

In all the struggles of his soul,

And all the strifes his soul abhorred,

She shone before him like a goal—

A shady bower of fresh reward—

A shallop riding in the mole,

That waited with obedient helm

To bear him over sparkling seas,

Into a new and fragrant realm,

Before the vigor of a breeze

That drove, but might not overwhelm.

IX.

To symmetry the oak is grown

Which all winds visit on the lea,

While that which lists the monotone

Of the long blast that sweeps the sea,

And answers to its breath alone,

Turns with aversion from the breeze,

And stretches all its stunted limbs

Landward and heavenward, toward the trees

That listen to a thousand hymns,

And grow to grander destinies.

Man may not live on whitest loaves,

With all of coarser good dismissed ;

He pines and starves who never roves

Beyond the holy eucharist,

To gather of the fields and groves.

And he who seeks to fill his heart

With solace of a single friend,

Will find refreshment but in part,

Or, sadder still, will find the end

Of all his reach of thought and art.

They who love best need friendship most ;

Hearts only thrive on varied good ;

And he who gathers from a host

Of friendly hearts his daily food,

Is the best friend that we can boast.

She left her husband with his friends ;
She called them round him at her board ;
And found their culture made amends
For all the time that, from her hoard,
She spared him for these nobler ends.

He was her lover ; that sufficed :
His home was in the Holy Place
With that of the Beloved Christ.
And friendship had no subtle grace
By which his love could be enticed.

Of all his friends, she was but one :
She held with them a common field.
Exclusive right—with love begun—
Ended with love, and stood repealed,
Leaving his friendship free to run

Toward man or woman, all unmissed.

She knew she had no right to bind

His friendship to her single wrist,

So long as love was true and kind,

And made her its monopolist.

No time was grudged with jealous greed

Which either books or friendship claimed.

He was her friend, and she had need

Of all—unhindered and unblamed—

That he could win, through word or deed.

Her friend waxed great as grew the man;

Her temple swelled as rose her priest—

With power to bless and right to ban;—

And all who served him, most or least,—

From chorister and sacristan

6

To those whose frankincense and myrrh

Perfumed the sacred courts with alms,—

Were gracious ministers to her,

Who found the largess in her palms,

And him the friendly almoner.

X.

The river of their life was one ;

The shores down which they passed were two ;

One mirrored mountains, huge and dun,

The other crimped the green and blue,

And sparkled in the kindly sun !

Twin barks, with answering flags, they move

With even canvas down the stream,

In smooth or ruffled waters grooved,

And found such islands in their dream

As rest and loving speech behooved.

Ah fair the goodly gardens smiled

On Philip at his rougher strand!

And grandly loomed the summits, isled

In seas of cloud, to her who scanned

From her far shore the lofty wild.

Two lives, two loves—both self-forgot

In loyal homage to their oath ;

Two lives, two loves, but living not

By ministry that reached them both,

In service of a common lot,

They sailed the stream ; and every mile

Broadened with beauty as they passed ;

And fruitful shore and trysting-isle,

And all love's intercourse were glassed

And blessed in Heaven's benignant smile.

LOVE'S CONSUMMATIONS.

THE summer passed, the autumn came ;
The world swung over toward the night ;
The forests robed themselves in flame,
Then faded slowly into white ;
And set within a crystal frame

Of frozen streams, the shaggy boles
Of oak and elm, with leafless crowns,
Were painted stark upon the knolls ;
And cots and villages and towns
On virgin canvas glowed like coals

In tawny red, or strove in vain

To shame the white in which they stood.

The fairest tint was but a stain

Upon the snow, that quenched the wood,

And paved the street, and draped the plain!

II.

Oh! Southern cheeks are quick to feel

The magic finger of the frost;

And Mildred heard but one long peal

From the fierce Arctic, which embossed

Her window-panes, and set the seal

Of cold on all her eye beheld,

When through her veins there swept new fire,

And, in her answering bosom, swelled

New purposes and new desire,

And force to higher deeds impelled.

Ah! well for her the languor cast
That followed from her Southern clime!
The time would come—was coming fast,—
Love's consummated, crowning time—
Of which her heart had antepast!

A strange new life was in her breast;
Her eyes were full of wondrous dreams;
She sailed all whiles from crest to crest
Of a broad ocean, through whose gleams
She saw an island wrapped in rest!

And as she drove across the sea,
Toward the fair port that fixed her gaze,
Her life was like a rosary,
Whose slowly counted beads were days
Of prayer for one that was to be!

III.

Oh roses, roses! Who shall sing

The beauty of the flowers of God!

Or thank the angel from whose wing

The seeds are scattered on the sod

From which such bloom and perfume spring!

Sure they have heavenly genesis

Which make a heaven of every place;

Which company our bale and bliss,

And never to our sinning race

Speak aught unhallowed, or amiss!

When love is grieved, their buds atone;

When love is wed, their forms are near;

They blend their breathing with the moan

Of love when dying, and the bier

Is white with them in every zone.

No spot is mean that they begem;

No nosegay fair that holds them not;

They melt the pride and stir the phlegm

Of lord and churl, in court and cot,

And weave a common diadem

For human brows where'er they grow.

They write all languages of red,

They speak all dialects of snow,

And all the words of gold arc said

With fragrant meanings where they blow i

Oh sweetest flowers! Oh flowers divine!

In which God comes so closely down,

We gather from his chosen sign

The tints that cluster in his crown—

The perfume of his breath benign!

Oh, sweetest flowers! Oh, flowers that hold

The fragrant life of Paradise

For a brief day, shut fold in fold,

That we may drink it in a trice,

And drop the empty pink and gold!

Oh sweetest flowers, that have a breath

For every passion that we feel!

That tell us what the Master saith

Of blessing, in our woe and weal,

And all events of life and death!

IV.

The time of roses came again;

And one had bloomed within the manse,—

Bloomed in a burst of midnight pain,

And plumed its life in fair expanse,

Beneath love's nursing sun and rain.

6*

Such tendance ne'er had flower before!

Such beauty ne'er had flower returned!

Found on that distant island-shore,

Whose secret she at last had learned,

And made her own for evermore,

Mildred consigned it to her breast;

And though she knew it took its hue

From her, it seemed the Lord's bequest,—

Still sparkling with the heavenly dew,

And still with heavenly beauty dressed.

Oh, roses! ye were wondrous fair

That summer by the river side!

For hearts were blooming everywhere,

In sympathy of love and pride,

With that which came to Mildred's care.

And rose as red as rose could be

Was Philip's heart with joy abloom,

That cast its fragrance far and free,

And filled his lonely, silent room

With rapture of paternity !

v.

The evening fell on field and street ;

The glow-worm lit his phosphor lamp,

For fairy forms and fairy feet,

That gathered for their nightly tramp

Where grass was green and flowers were sweet.

In devious circles, round and round,

The night-hawk coursed the twilight sky,

Or shot like lightning the profound,

With breezy thunder in the cry

That marked his furious rebound !

The zephyrs breathed through elm and ash,

From new-mown hay and heliotrope,

And came through Philip's open sash

With sheen of stars that lit the cope,

And twinkling of the fire-fly's flash.

He heard the baby's weary plaint;

He heard the mother's soothing words;

And sitting in his hushed restraint,

One voice was murmur of the birds,

And one the hymning of a saint!

And as he sat alone, immersed

In the fond fancies of the time,

Her voice in mellow music burst,

And by a rhythmic stair of rhyme

Led down to sleep the child she nursed.

"Rockaby, lullaby, bees on the clover!—

Crooning so drowsily, crying so low—

Rockaby, lullaby, dear little rover!

Down into wonderland—

Down to the under-land—

Go, oh go!

Down into wonderland go!

"Rockaby, lullaby, rain on the clover!

Tears on the eyelids that struggle and weep!

Rockaby, lullaby—bending it over!

Down on the mother world,

Down on the other world!

Sleep, oh sleep!

Down on the mother-world sleep!

"Rockaby, lullaby, dew on the clover!

Dew on the eyes that will sparkle at dawn!

Rockaby, lullaby, dear little rover!

Into the stilly world !

Into the lily world,

Gone ! oh gone !

Into the lily world, gone ! "

VI.

They sprouted like the prophet's gourd ;

They grew within a single night ;

So swift his busy years were scored

That, ere he knew, his hope was white

With harvest bending round his board !

And eyes were black and eyes were blue,

And blood of mother and of sire,

Each to its native humor true,

Blent Northern force with Southern fire

In strength and beauty, strange and new.

The Gallic brown, the Saxon snow,

The raven locks, the flaxen curls,

Were so commingled in the flow

Of the new blood of boys and girls,

That Puritan and Huguenot

In love's alembic were advanced

To higher types and finer forms;

And ardent humors thrilled and danced

Through veins that tempered all their storms,

Or held them in restraint entranced.

Oh! many times, as flew the years,

The dainty cradle-song was sung;

And bore its balm to restless ears,

As one by one the nested young

Slept in their willows and their tears.

To each within the reedy glade,

Hid from some tyrant's cruel schemes,

It was a princess, or her maid,

Who bore him to the realm of dreams,

And made him seer by accolade

Of flaming bush and parted deep,

Of gushing rocks and raining corn,

And fire and cloud, and lengthened sweep

Of thousands toward the promised morn,

Across the wilderness of sleep!

VII.

The years rolled on in grand routine

Of useful toil and chastening care,

Till Philip, grown to heights serene

Of conscious power, and ripe with prayer,

Took on the strong and stately mien

Of one on whom had been conferred

The doing of a knightly deed;

And waited till it bade him gird

The harness on him and his steed,

For man and for his Master's word.

His name was spoken far and near,

And sounded sweet on every tongue;

Men knew him only to revere,

And those who knew him nearest, flung

Their hearts before his grand career,

And paved his way with loyal trust.

He was their strongest, noblest man,—

Sworn foe of every selfish lust,

And brave to do as wise to plan,

And swift to judge as pure and just.

VIII.

Against such foil the mistress stood—
A pearl upon a cross of gold—
White with consistent womanhood,
And fixed with unrelaxing hold
Upon the centre of the rood!

Through all those years of loving thrift,
Nor blame nor discord marred their lot;
Each to the lover-life was gift;
And each was free from blur or blot
That called for silence or for shrift.

Both bore the burden they upheld
With patient hands along the road;
And though, with passing years, it swelled
Until it grew a weary load,
Nor tongue complained, nor heart rebelled.

At length the time of trial came,

And they were tried as gold is tried.

Their peace of life went up in flame,

And what was good was vilified,

And what was blameless came to blame.

IX.

The Southern sky was dun with cloud;

And looming lurid o'er its edge

The brows of awful forms were bowed,

That forged in flame the fateful wedge

Which waited in the angry shroud.

The banner of the storm unfurled,

And all the powers of death arrayed

In black battalions, to be hurled

Down through the rack—a blazing blade—

To cleave the realm, and shake the world!

The North was full of nameless dread;

Wild portents flamed from out the pole;

Old scars on Freedom's bosom bled,

And sick at heart and vexed of soul

She tossed in fever on her bed!

Pale Commerce hid her face and whined;

The arms of Toil were paralyzed;

The wise were of divided mind,

And they who counselled and advised

Were sightless leaders of the blind.

Men lost their faith in good and great;

No captain sprang, or prophet-bard,

To win their trust, and save the state

From the wild storm that, like a pard,

On quivering haunches lay in wait!

The loyal only were not brave;

E'en Peace became a cringing dog;

The patriot paltered like a knave,

And partisan and demagogue

Quarrelled o'er Freedom's waiting grave.

X.

Amid the turmoil and disgrace,

The voice was clear, from first to last,

Of one who, in the desert place

Of barren counsels, held him fast

His shepherd's crook, and made it mace

To bear before the Great Event

Whose harbinger he chose to be,

And called on all men to repent,

And build a way from sea to sea,

For Freedom's full enfranchisement.

For Philip, to his conscience leal,

Conceived that God had chosen him

With Treason's sophistries to deal,

And grapple with the Anakim

Whose menace shook the commonweaL

His pulpit smoked beneath his blows;

His voice was heard in hall and street;

A thousand friends became his foes,

And pews were empty or replete,

With passion's ebbs and overflows.

They trailed his good name in the mire;

They spat their venom in his eyes;

They taunted him with mad desire

For power, and gathered his replies

In braver words and fiercer fire.

He was a wolf, disguised in wool ;

He was a viper in the breast ;

He was a villain, or the tool

Of greater villains ; at the best,

A blind enthusiast and fool!

As swelled the tempest, rose the man ;

He turned to sport their brutal spleen ;

And none could choose be slow to span

The difference that lay between

A Prospero and a Caliban!

XI.

She would not move him otherwise,

Although her heart was sad and sore.

That which was venal in his eyes

To her a lovely aspect wore,

And helped to weave the thousand ties

Which bound her to her youth, and all

The loves that she had left behind

When, from her father's stately hall,

She came, her Northern home to find,

With him who held her heart in thrall.

In the dark pictures which he drew

Of instituted shame and wrong,

She saw no figures that she knew,

But a confused and hateful throng

Of forms that in his fancy grew.

Her father's rule, benign and mild,

Was all of slavery she had known;

To her, an Afric was a child—

A charge in other ages thrown

On Christian honor, from the wild

Of savagery in which the Fates

Had given him birth and dwelling-place—

And so, descending through estates

Of gentle vassalage, his race

Had come to men of later dates.

Black hands her baby form had dressed;

Black hands her blacker hair had curled;

And she had found a dusky breast

The sweetest breast in all the world

When she was thirsty or at rest.

There was no touch of memory's chords—

No picture on her blooming wall,—

Of life upon the sunny swards

They reproduced,—but brought recall

Of happy slaves and gentle lords.

7

And Philip charged a deadly sin
Upon that beautiful domain,
Condemning all who dwelt therein,
And branding with the awful stain
Her friends, and all her dearest kin.

Yet still she knew his conscience clear,—
That he believed his voice was God's;
And listened with a voiceless fear
To the portentous periods
In which he preached the chosen year

Of expiation and release,
And prophesied that Slavery's power,
Grown great apace with crime's increase,
Before the front of Right should cower,
And bid God's people go in peace!

XII.

The fierce invectives of his tongue
Frayed every day her wounds afresh,
And with new pain her bosom wrung,
For they envenomed kindred flesh,
To which in sympathy she clung.

Yet not a finger did she lift
To hold him from his fateful task,
Though Satan oft essayed to sift
Her soul as wheat, and bade her ask
Somewhat from conscience as a gift.

And when a serpent in his slime
Crept to her ear with phrase polite,
Prating of duty to her time
And to her people—swift and white
She turned and cursed him for his crime!

She would have naught of all the brood
Of temporizing, drivelling shows
Of men who Philip's words withstood :
Against them all her love uprose,
And all her pride of womanhood.

She loved her kindred none the less,
She loved her husband still the more,
For well she knew that with distress
He saw the heavy cross she bore
With steadfast faith and tenderness.

No strife of jarring policies,
No conflict of embittered states,
No chart, defining by degrees
Of latitude her country's hates,
Could change her friends to enemies.

The motives ranged on either hand,

Behind the war of word and will,

Were such as she could understand

And, with respect to all, fulfil

Love's broad and beautiful command.

So, with all questions hushed to sleep,

And all opinions put aside,

She gave her loved ones to the keep

Of God, whatever should betide,

To bear her joy or bid her weep!

XIII.

Though Philip knew he wounded her,

His faith to God and faith to man

Bade him go forward, and incur

Such cost as, since the world began,

Has burdened Freedom's harbinger.

No heart or hand was his to flinch

From ease or reputation lost;

Nor waste of gold, nor hunger-pinch,

Nor e'en his home's black holocaust,

Could stay his arm. Though inch by inch,

The maddened hosts of scorn and scath

Should crowd him backward to defeat,

He would but strive with sterner wrath,

And bless the hand that, soft and sweet,

Withheld its hinderance from his path!

XIV.

Still darker loomed the Southern cloud,

While o'er its black and billowed face

In furrowed fire the lightning ploughed,

And ramping from his hiding-place

Roared the wild Thunder, fierce and loud!

And still men chattered of their trade,

And strove to banish their alarms;

And some were puzzled, some afraid,

And some held up their feeble arms

In indignation while they prayed!

And others weakly talked of schism

As boon of God in place of war,

And bared their foreheads for its chrism!

While direr than the mace of Thor,

In mid-air hung the cataclysm

Which waited but some chance, or act,

To shiver the electric spell,

And pour in one fierce cataract

A rain of blood and fire of hell

On Freedom's temple spoiled and sacked.

The politician plied his craft;

The demagogue still schemed and lied;

The patriot wept, the traitor laughed;

The coward to his covert hied,

And statesmen went distract or daft.

Contention raged in Senate halls;

Confusion reigned in field and town;

High conclaves flattened into brawls,

And till and hammer, smock and gown,

Nor duty knew nor heard its calls!

XV.

At last, incontinent of fire,

The cloud of menace belched its brand;

And every state and every shire

And town and hamlet in the land,

Shook with the smiting of its ire!

Men looked each other in the eyes,

And beat their burning breasts and cursed !

At last the silliest were wise ;

And swift to flash and thunder-burst

Fashioned in anger their replies.

The smoke of Sumter filled the air.

Men breathed it in in one long breath ;

And straight upspringing everywhere,

Life burgeoned on the mounds of death,

And bloomed in valleys of despair.

The fire of Sumter, fierce and hot,

Welded their purpose into one ;

And discord hushed, and strife forgot,

They swore that what had thus begun

With sacrilegious cannon-shot,

7*

Should find in analogue of flame

Such answer of the nation's host,

That the old flag, washed clean from shame

In blood, should wave from coast to coast,

Over one realm in heart and name!

XVI.

Pale doubters, scourged by countless whips,

Fled to their refuge, or obeyed

The motives and the masterships

That time and circumstance betrayed

Through Patriotism's apocalypse,

And, sympathetic with the spasm

Of loyal life that thrilled the clime,

Lost in the swift enthusiasm

The loose intention of their crime;

Then leaped in swarms the awful chasm

That held them parted from the mass.

The North was one in heart and thought,

And that which could not come to pass

Through loyal eloquence, was wrought

By one hot word from lips of brass!

XVII.

The cry sprang upward and sped on :

" To arms! for freedom and the flag!"

And swift, from Maine to Oregon,

O'er glebe and lake and mountain-crag,

Hurtled the fierce Euroclydon.

Men dropped their mallets on the bench,

Forsook their ploughs on hill and plain,

And tore themselves, with piteous wrench

Of heart and hope, from love and gain,

And trooped in throngs to tent and trench.

"To arms!" and Philip heard the cry.

Not his the valor cheap and small

To bluster with brave phrase, and fly

When trumpet blare and rifle-ball

Proclaimed the time for words gone by!

Men knew their chieftain. He had borne

Their insolence through struggling years,

And they—the dastards, the forsworn—

Who had ransacked the hemispheres

For instruments to wreak their scorn

On him and all of kindred speech,

Gathered around him with his friends,

And with stern plaudits heard him preach

A gospel whose stupendous ends

Their martyred blood could only reach.

They gave him honor far and wide,

As one who backed his word by deed;

And he whose task had been to guide,

Was chosen by acclaim to lead

The men who gathered at his side.

The crook was banished for the glave;

The churchman's black for soldier-blue;

The man of peace became a brave;

And, in the dawn of conflict, drew

His sword his country's life to save.

XIX.

They came from mead and mountain-top;

They came from factory and forge;

And one by one, from farm and shop—

Still gravel to the Northman's gorge—

Followed the servile Ethiop.

Gaunt, grimy men, whose ways had been

Among the shadows and the slums,

With pedagogue and paladin,

Rushed, at the rolling of the drums,

To Philip, and were mustered in !

The beat of drum and scream of fife,

Commingling with the thundering tramp

Of trooping throngs, so changed the life

Of the calm village that the camp,

And what it prophesied of strife,

And hap of loss and hap of gain,

Became of every tongue the theme ;

Till burning heart and throbbing brain

Could waking think, and sleeping dream,

Of naught but battles and the slain.

XX.

With eager eyes and helpful hands
The women met in solemn crowds,
And shred the linen into bands
That had been better saved for shrouds,
Or want's imperious demands.

And with them all sad Mildred walked,
The bearer of a heavy cross ;
For at her side the phantom stalked—
Nor left her for an hour—of loss
Which by no fortune might be balked.

For one or all she loved must fall ;
One cause must perish in defeat ;
Success of either would appall,
And victory, however sweet
To others, would to her be gall.

To each, with equal heart allied,

Her love was like the love of God,

That wraps the country in its tide,

And o'er its hosts, benign and broad,

Broods with its pity and its pride !

A thousand chances of the feud

She wove and ravelled one by one,—

Of hands in kindred blood imbrued,—

Of father, face to face with son,

And friends turned foemen fierce and rude.

And in her dreams two forms were met,

Of friends as leal as ever breathed—

Her husband and her brother—wet

With priceless blood from swords ensheathed

In hearts that loved each other yet !

But itching ears her language scanned,

And jealous eyes were on her steps;

And fancies into rumors fanned

By loyal shrews and demireps

Proclaimed her traitress to the land.

They knew her blood, but could not know

That mighty passion of her heart

Which, reaching widely in its woe,

Grasped all she loved on either part,

And could not, would not let it go!

XXI.

The time of gathering came and went—

Of noisy zeal and hasty drill—

And everywhere, in field and tent,—

A constant presence,—Philip's will

Moulded the callow regiment.

And then there fell a gala day,

When all the mighty, motley swarm

Appeared in beautiful display

Of burnished arms and uniform,

And gloried in their brave array!—

And, later still, the hour of dread

To all the simple country round,

When forth, with Philip at their head,

They marched from the familiar ground,

And drained its life, and left it dead;—

Dead but for those who pined with grief;

Dead but for fears that could not die;

Dead as the world when flower and leaf

Are still beneath a gathering sky,

And ocean sleeps on reach and reef.

The weary waiting time had come,

When only apprehension waked ;

And lonely wives sat chill and dumb

Among their broods, with hearts that ached

And echoed the retreating drum.

Teachers forgot to preach their creeds,

And trade forsook its merchandise ;

The fallow fields grew rank with weeds,

And none had interest or eyes

For aught but war's ensanguined deeds.

As one who lingered by a bier

Where all she loved lay dead and cold,

Sad Mildred sat without a tear,

Living again the days of old,

Or, with the vision of a seer,

Forecasting the disastrous end.

Whate'er might come, she did not dare

Believe that fortune would defend

The noble life she could not spare,

And save her lover and her friend.

Her blooming girls and stalwart boys

Could never comprehend the woe

Which dropped its measure of their joys,

And felt but horror in the show,

And heard but murder in the noise,

And dreamed of death when stillness fell

Behind the gay and shouting corps.

They saw her haunted by the spell

Of a great sorrow, and forebore

To question griefs they could not quell.

Small time she gave to vain regret ;

Brief space to thought of that adieu

Which crushed her breast, when last they met,

And in love's baptism bathed anew

Cheeks, lips, and eyes, and left them wet !

In deeds of sympathy and grace,

She moved among the homes forlorn,

Alike to beautiful and base

And to the stricken and the shorn,

The guardian angel of the place.

XXII.

Oh piteous waste of hopes and fears !

Oh cruel stretch of long delay !

Oh homes bereft ! Oh useless tears !

Oh war ! that ravened on its prey

Through Pain's immeasurable years !

The town was mourning for its dead ;

The streets were black with widowhood ;

While orphaned children begged for bread,

And Rachel, for the brave and good,

Mourned, and would not be comforted.

The regiment that, straight and crisp,

Shone like a wheat-field in the sun,

Its swift voice deafened to a lisp,

Fell, ere the war was well begun,

And waned and withered to a wisp.

And Philip, grown to higher rank,

Crowned with the bays of splendid deeds

Of the full cup of glory drank,

And lived, though all his reeking steeds

In the red front of conflict sank.

The star of conquest waxed or waned,

Yet still the call came back for men ;

Still the lamenting town was drained,

And still again, and still again,

Till only impotence remained !

XXIII.

There came at length an eve of gloom—

Dread Gettysburg's eventful eve—

When all the gathering clouds of doom

Hung low, the breathless air to cleave

With scream of shell and cannon-boom !

Man knew too well, and woman felt

That when the next wild morn should rise,

A blow of battle would be dealt

Before whose fire ten thousand eyes—

As in a furnace flame—would melt.

And on this eve—her flock asleep—

Knelt Mildred at her lonely bed.

She could not pray, she did not weep,

But only moaned, and, moaning, said:

"Oh God! he sows what I must reap!

"He will not live: he must not die!

But oh, my poor, prophetic heart!

It warns me that there lingers nigh

The hour when love and I must part!"

And then she startled with a cry,

For, from beneath her lattice, came

A low and once repeated call!

She knew the voice that spoke her name,

And swiftly through the midnight hall

She fluttered noiseless as a flame,

And on its unresisting hinge
Threw wide her hospitable door,
To one whose spirit could not cringe
Though he was shelterless, and bore
No right her freedom to infringe.

She wildly clasped his neck of bronze ;
She rained her kisses on his face,
Grown tawny with a thousand suns,
And holding him in her embrace,
She led him to her little ones,

Who, reckless of his coming, slept.
Then down the stair with silent feet
And through the shadowy hall she swept,
And saw, between her and the street,
A form that into darkness crept.

8

She closed the door with speechless dread;

She fixed the bolt with trembling hand;

Then led the rebel to his bed,

Whom love and safety had unmanned,

And left him less alive than dead.

Through nights and days of fear and grief,

She kept her faithful watch and ward,

But love and rest brought no relief;

And all he begged for of his Lord

Was death, with passion faint and brief.

XXIV.

Around the house were prying eyes,

And gossips hiding under trees;

And Mildred heard the steps of spies

At midnight, when, upon her knees,

She sought the comfort of the skies.

Strange voices rose upon the night;

Strange errands entered at the gate;

Her hours were months of pale affright;

Though still her prisoner of state

Was shielded from their eager sight.

And there were hirelings in pursuit,

Who thirsted for his golden price;

And, swift allied with pimp and brute,

And quick to purchase and entice,

They found the tree that held their fruit.

XXV.

The day of Gettysburg had set;

The smoke had drifted from the scene,

And burnished sword and bayonet

Lay rusting where, but yestere'en,

They dropped with life-blood red and wet!

The swift invader had retraced
His march, and left his fallen braves,
Covered at night in voiceless haste,
To sleep in memorable graves,
But knew that all his loss was waste.

The nation's legions, stretching wide,
Too sore to chase, too weak to cheer,
Gave sepulture to those who died,
And saw their foemen disappear
Without the loss of power or pride.

And then, swift-sweeping like a gale,
Through all the land, from end to end,
Grief poured its wild, untempered wail,
And father, mother, wife, and friend
Forgot their country in their bale.

And Philip, with his fatal wound,

Was borne beyond the battle's blaze,

Across the torn and quaking ground,

His ear too dull to heed the praise,

That spoke him hero, robed and crowned.

They bent above his blackened face,

And questioned of his last desire ;

And with his old, familiar grace,

And smiling mouth, and eye of fire,

He answered them : " My wife's embrace ! "

They wiped his forehead of its stain,

They bore him tenderly away,

Through teeming mart and wide champaign,

Till on a twilight, cool and gray,

And wet with weeping of the rain,

They gave him to a silent crowd

That waited at the river's marge,

Of men with age and sorrow bowed,

Who raised and bore their precious charge,

Through groups that watched and wailed aloud.

XXVI.

The hounds of power were at her gate ;

And at their heels, a yelping pack

Of graceless mongrels stood in wait,

To mark the issue of attack,

With lips that slavered with their hate.

With window raised and portal barred,

The mistress scanned the darkening space,

And with a visage hot and hard—

At bay before the cruel chase—

She held them in her fierce regard.

" What would ye—spies and hirelings—what ? "

  She asked with accent, stern and brave ;

" Why come ye to this sacred spot,

  Led by the counsel of a knave,

  And flanked by slanderer and sot ?

" You have my husband : has he earned

  No meed of courtesy for me ?

  Is this the recompense returned,

  That she he loved the best should be

  Suspected, persecuted, spurned ?

" My home is wrecked : what would ye more ?

  My life is ruined—what new boon ?

  My children's hearts are sad and sore

  With weeping for the wounds that soon

  Will plead for healing at my door !

"I hold your prisoner—stand assured :

Safe from his foes : aye, safe from you!—

Safe in a sister's love immured,

And by a warden kept as true

As e'er the test of faith endured.

"Why, men, he was my brother born!

My hero, all my youthful years!

My counsellor, to guide and warn!

My shield alike from foes and fears!

And when he came to me, forlorn,

"What could I do but hail him guest,

And bind his cruel wounds with balm,

And give him on his sister's breast

That which he asked, the humble alm

Of a safe pillow where to rest?

"Come, then, and dare the wrath of fate!

Come, if you must, or if you will!

But know that I am desperate;

And shafts that wound, and wounds that kill

Your deed of dastardy await!"

A murmur swept through all the mob;

The base informer slunk afar;

And lusty cheer and stifled sob

Rose to her at the window-bar,

While those whose hands were come to rob

Her dwelling of its treasure, cursed;

For round their heads the menace flew

That he who dared adventure first,

Or first an arm of murder drew,

Should taste of vengeance at its worst.
    8*

XXVII.

A heavy tramp, a murmuring sound,

Low mingling with the murmuring rain,—

Heard in the wind and in the ground,—

Came up the street—a tide of pain,

In which the angry din was drowned.

The leaders of the tumult fled ;

The door flew open with a crash ;

And down the street wild Mildred sped,

Piercing the darkness like a flash,

And walked beside her husband's bed.

Slowly the solemn train advanced ;

The crowd fell back with parted ranks ;

And like a giant, half entranced,

Sailing between strange, spectral banks,

From side to side the soldier glanced.

The sobbing rain, the evening dim,

The dusky forms that pushed and peered,

The swaying couch, the aching limb,

The lights and shadows, sharp and weird,

Were but a troubled dream to him.

He knew his love—all else unknown,

Or seen through reason's sad eclipse—

And with her hand within his own,

Or fondly pressed upon his lips,

He clung to it, as if alone

It had the power to stay his feet

Yet longer on the verge of life;

And thus they vanished from the street—

The shepherd-warrior and his wife—

Within the manse's closed retreat.

XXVIII.

Embraced by home, his soul grew light;

And though he moaned: " My head! my head!"

His life turned back its outward flight,

Like his, who, from the prophet's bed,

Startled the wondering Shunammite.

He greeted all with tender speech;

He told his children he should die;

He gave his fond farewell to each,

With messages, and fond good-by

To all he loved beyond his reach.

And then he spoke her brother's name:

" Tell him," he said, " that, in my death,

I cherished his untarnished fame,

And, to my life's expiring breath,

Held his brave spirit free from blame.

" We strove alike for truth's behoof,

With honest faith and love sincere,—

For God and country, right and roof,

And issues that do not appear,

But wait with Heaven the awful proof."

A tottering figure reached the door ;

The brother fell upon the bed,

And, in each other's arms once more,

With breast to breast, and head to head,—

Twin barks, they drifted from the shore ;

And backward on the sobbing air

Came the same words from warring lips :

" God save my country ! " and the prayer

Still wailing from the drifting ships,

Returned in measures of despair ;

Till far, at the horizon's verge

They passed beyond the tearful eyes

That could not know if in the surge

They sank at last, or in the skies

Forgot the burden of their dirge !

XXIX.

In Northern blue and Southern brown,

Twin coffins and a single grave,

They laid the weary warriors down ;

And hands that strove to slay and save

Had equal rest and like renown.

For in the graveyard's hallowed close

A woman's love made neutral soil,

Where it might lay the forms of those

Who, resting from their fateful broil,

Had ceased forever to be foes.

To her and those who clung to her—
From manly eldest down to least—
The obsequies, the sepulchre,
The chanting choir, the weeping priest,
And all the throng and all the stir

Of sympathetic country-folk,
And all the signs of death and dole,
Were but a dream that beat and broke
In chilling waves on heart and soul,
Till in the silence they awoke.

She was a widow, and she wept;
She was a mother, and she smiled;
Her faith with those she loved was kept,
Though still the war-cry, fierce and wild,
Around the harried country swept.

No more with this had she to do;

God and her little ones were left;

And unto these, serene and true,

She gave the life so soon bereft

Of its first gifts, and rose anew

At duty's call to make amends

For all her loss of loves and lands;

And found, to speed her noble ends,

The succor of uplifting hands,

And solace of a thousand friends.

And o'er her precious graves she built

A stone whereon the yellow boss

Of sword on sword with naked hilt

Lay as the symbol of her cross,

In mournful meaning, carved and gilt.

And underneath were graved the lines :—

" THEY DID THE DUTY THAT THEY SAW ;

BOTH WROUGHT AT GOD'S SUPREME DESIGNS

AND, UNDER LOVE'S ETERNAL LAW,

EACH LIFE WITH EQUAL BEAUTY SHINES."

XXX.

Peace, with its large and lilied calms,

Like moonlight sleeps on land and lake,

With healing in its dewy balms,

For pride that pines and hearts that ache,

From Huron to the land of palms!

From rock-bound Massachusetts Bay

To California's Golden Gate ;

From where Itasca's waters play,

To those which plunge or palpitate

A thousand happy leagues away.

And drink, among her dunes and bars,

The Mississippi's boiling tide,

Still floating from a million spars,

The nation's ensign, undefied,

Blazons its galaxy of stars.

No more to party strife the slave,

And freed from Hate's infernal spells,

Love pays her tribute to the brave,

And snows her holy immortelles

O'er friend and foe, where'er his grave.

On every Decoration Day

Each pilgrim to her hallowed grounds

Brings tribute of a flower or spray;

And white-haired Mildred finds her mounds

Decked with the garnered bloom of May.

And Philip's first-born, strong and sage,

(Through Heaven's design or happy chance)

Finds the old church his heritage ;

And still, The Mistress of the Manse,

Sits Mildred, in her silver age !

END.